Banna and **Bree**
Blown to
Borneo

Book Three

Banna and **Bree**
Blown to
Borneo

Karen Cross

Chapter 1

Deep in the swampy grasslands of the Okavango Delta lived two baboons called Banna and Bree. They lived in a troupe of chacma baboons. Every day they rolled in the grass, bounded from tree to tree, and from bush to bush, hiding in the lush foliage at the first sign of danger.

It was here in the Delta where the zebras grazed, sharing the grass with the wildebeest. Elephants plodded along in breeding herds, the little ones tucked under their mothers' tummies.

1

Giraffes loped gently across the savannahs, often passing on the way a pride of lions lazing under the trees.

Banna and Bree looked forward to fun and adventure and rose with the sun each and every morning so that they could play together and see what the day brought them. Life was good.

In the Delta, the water flowed down from the wet season in Angola and flooded the dry plains every year. The new waterways created a bountiful oasis for the animals after a long, dry season. Excited by the abundance of water, the elephants playfully sprayed each other. The hippos wallowed, their eyes just above the water, flapping their ears and snorting the air out of their lungs.

On this particular day, Banna and Bree were playing in the savannah with the other baboons when the bright oranges of the setting sky started to darken and the leaves on the ground began to spin.

"Adventure calls!" cried Banna. Hand in hand they approached the whirlwind of leaves and dust, their hearts beating wildly. It had been months since Banna and Bree had been on an adventure, and they were both keen to see where the next one would take them. Suddenly everything became quiet and still.

The cloud shaped like a beautiful lady appeared before them. She had her hands clasped in front of her and a warm smile on her face, just like the last time they had seen her. Her smile was soothing and as she spoke, they stood mesmerised.

"Banna and Bree, I am so pleased to see you, and happy that you chose to come to me again. I have so much more of our beautiful planet to show you. The world is full of adventure with so many unique animals and wonderful environments to see. Shut your eyes and get ready for your next adventure."

Banna and Bree closed their eyes, raised their arms, and felt the familiar sensation of being lifted into the air. The cloud lady whispered, "Enjoy yourselves, Banna and Bree."

After the spinning had slowed, Banna and Bree opened their eyes and felt the calm and quiet around them. They found themselves lying on

3

the ground and slowly opened their eyes. The bush was dense, the leaves were green, and the air was warm. There were birds calling and they could hear the constant chatter of monkeys.

"I hear monkeys," whispered Bree. "Maybe we are going back to see Jastin."

"Not unless Jastin's nose has become a lot longer and he has turned orange," whispered Banna, pointing to the funniest looking creature who was watching their every move.

"I'm not sure that is a monkey," replied Bree. "It is bigger than the monkeys we have seen, and it's also bigger than us baboons."

"The colouring is weird, too," whispered Banna. "I haven't seen an orange monkey before, and I haven't seen a nose that big before either."

Still lying on the ground, they continued to look around them. They saw more of the orange creatures in the trees.

As Bree and Banna watched the creatures manoeuvre themselves through the trees, they started to become a little uneasy. The orange monkeys were now surrounding them and none of them had a smile or a welcoming wave.

Before they realised what was going on, two of the orange monkeys were on top of them and pinning them to the ground. They held Banna and Bree's arms behind their backs, while another two tightly bound their hands together so they could not move.

They were outnumbered, unable to move their arms, and now their feet were being tied up with vines. Two of the large orange monkeys lifted them up and carried them to an open area. Many other animals were now watching them.

Banna called out in a friendly tone, "Hi, my name is Banna and this is my friend Bree."

They ignored Banna, and the biggest of the orange monkeys yelled at the other monkeys like he was the leader. His nose wobbled on his face as he spoke sternly to them.

"What are you, and why have you come into a protected area of the forest?" yelled the largest of the monkeys at Banna and Bree.

"You do not live here!" yelled another.

"We have never seen you in this part of the forest!" screamed another monkey.

"We are baboons," replied Bree nervously.

"We have come here from the Okavango Delta in Botswana to meet new animals and learn from you."

"Who do you report to?" asked the monkey, getting angry and agitated. "What do you plan to learn?" He raised his bushy eyebrows.

"We don't report to anybody," Banna tried to explain. "We are here on a holiday."

"A holiday?" repeated the leader of the orange monkeys sarcastically. "Do you see any resorts here?"

"We aren't interested in resorts or fancy holiday places," said Banna, trying to reason with him. "We were sent here by the wind to meet the animals and see the unique countryside."

Banna realised how silly it sounded as soon as he had finished speaking.

"The wind sent them here? They sound crazy!" screamed the large orange monkey to the others. "Tie them to the tree while we find Honey the Hornbill for her advice."

The orange monkeys all disappeared into the forest leaving Banna and Bree tied to a tree.

Chapter 2

A beautiful bird flew into the clearing, and landed next to Banna and Bree, who were still tied to the tree. The orange monkeys came back into the clearing as well.

"Why have you come to our forest?" asked the bird gracefully.

"We tried to tell the orange monkey," said Banna urgently.

"Orange monkey?" yelled the orange monkey.

"Let them continue," said the beautiful bird. The orange monkey put his hands on his hips,

7

he was not happy with Banna.

"We met a beautiful cloud lady who sent us here on the wind. Bree and I have been on adventures to other lands before. We are from Botswana in Africa."

"Aah-ha," nodded the bird.

"We are only interested in adventures," cried Bree desperately. "On our last adventure we went to the Great Barrier Reef in Australia. There was a cyclone and we met a koala, turtles, and a kangaroo family."

"Aah-ha," nodded the bird again.

"Please, we don't want to harm anybody," begged Banna. "We have been sent here, so it means we have come to a place that is unique and special."

"Aah-ha," nodded the bird for the third time. "Interesting."

The monkey leader looked intensely at the bird.

"They are telling the truth," said the bird to the orange monkey.

"We are telling the truth!" cried out Banna and Bree at the same time.

"Yes, I read faces and body language," said the bird. "It is a special gift. I can tell if someone is not telling the truth."

The orange monkey spoke softly. "We have to be careful who roams in our jungle as we are a protected forest and there are many bad things that can happen to us. There are plantations around us that are not protected."

"Where are we?" asked Bree, as gently as she could.

"You are in the Kabili Sepilok Forest Reserve in Sabah, which is in Borneo," said the bird. "Borneo has some of the most unique animals in the world. Some of us, like the proboscis monkey, are only found here, in Borneo. You won't find his species anywhere else in the world."

"We have been sent to some beautiful, unique places, and they have had some endangered species there as well," said Bree. "We went to Australia and swam in the Great Barrier Reef. It is the biggest coral reef system on our planet; you can even see it from the moon."

"I've heard about beautiful Australia and the Great Barrier Reef," said Hope, another hornbill.

"You two went swimming? Remember, Honey can tell if you are telling the truth. You don't look like swimmers."

"We had a little bit of help from some turtles," said Bree, smiling.

"The cloud lady sends us to the most amazing places on the planet to show us how animals and our environments are being treated," said Banna.

"My name is Pedro," interrupted the orange monkey leader, puffing out his chest. I am the leader of the proboscis monkeys in this reserve."

"Nice to meet you Pedro," said Bree. "We don't mean you any harm, and would love to get to know you all if you would let us."

"Are you like the other monkeys?" asked Banna, trying to engage him in conversation.

"As you may notice we look different to other monkeys," said Paige, another one of the proboscis monkeys. "We are orange and the males have a larger nose that I think looks rather distinguished."

Banna and Bree looked at the huge nose on Pedro's face, which wobbled when he spoke.

Paige's nose was a lot smaller and didn't wobble as much.

"We are nearly as big as people and we are powerful, yet graceful when we move through the trees," said Pedro with his chest still puffed out in pride.

"As well as the proboscis monkey, Borneo is home to the pygmy elephants, orangutans and the hornbill," said Paige. "But our forests continue to be cut or burned down, and we don't have a lot of it left for the animals that rely on this habitat."

"As we have said, we are not here to hurt you," said Banna. Please untie us; my hands are starting to go numb."

"Yes, of course," said Pedro. "You are no threat to us; where are my manners?"

Chapter 3

Pedro untied Banna and Bree. They moved to sit with Pedro and Paige in the clearing, with all the other animals that had gathered while they were tied up. Bree sat next to a huge male orangutan called Rupsa. He was the male orangutan in the area. A little orangutan crawled over and cuddled its mother tightly as she listened to the conversation.

"Why do they cut or burn your forests down when the animals need it for their homes?" asked Banna.

"Many years ago, Borneo consisted of majestic jungles and vast, dense forests of trees filled with numerous species," explained Pedro. "Then, sadly, people found out how well the palm oil sold and started to burn, log and clear the rainforest to plant palm oil trees."

"People who farm the plantations consider orangutans and pygmy elephants pests," said Honey. "They will go to any lengths to get rid of them, often killing and dumping them."

"Quite a number of animals now live in reserves like this one," said Paige. "They are protected by human rangers; their government has made the reserves a safe place for animals."

"Many other animals choose to live in the rainforests where their families have lived for many years," said Pedro, "but the unprotected rainforests can be dangerous at times."

"Why is palm oil so important?" asked Bree.

"The people make products like biscuits, chips, shampoo, chocolates, skin care and beauty products from the fruit of the palm oil tree," answered Rupsa.

"They get a lot of money for producing palm

oil," said Honey the Hornbill, shaking her head. "But this is also the type of forest environment that animals such as orangutans like to live in."

"My species are endangered," added Rupsa. "Do you know what that means?"

"Sadly we do, Rupsa," answered Bree. "We met some mountain gorillas in Rwanda that were endangered as well."

"I have heard stories about the Mountain Gorillas," said Rupsa. "Are they as big as trees?"

Bree laughed. "Not as big as trees, but they are large, gentle giants who just want to live in peace with their families."

"Just like the orangutan," said Rupsa quietly.

"We learned first-hand about the poachers and habitat destruction when we were in Rwanda," said Banna. "The poachers sell the Mountain Gorilla's body parts on the black market."

"That is very sad," said Pedro. "We have poachers in Borneo, as well as the illegal pet trade, where they sell live animals to people all over the world. They seem to target the orangutans that they find in their plantations."

Honey shook her head again in disappointment.

15

"I'm sorry for the way we tied you up, but we are very protective of our reserve," said Pedro. "Come and have some food with us."

The two baboons were very grateful for the food as they hadn't eaten in a while. They sat down to a feast of leaves, shoots, seeds and fruit with Pedro and the animals of the reserve who welcomed Banna and Bree into their family.

Bree and Banna talked into the night with the proboscis monkeys, the orangutans and the hornbills and quickly became friends. They told them stories of their adventures in Botswana and the animals told them about life in Borneo.

Chapter 4

For days, Bree and Banna helped the forest families gather food and watch over the younger ones. They met Esther, the pygmy elephant, and her baby Emme, who loved to follow Banna and Bree around and talk to them.

"We have elephants like you in Africa," Bree told Emme. "But they are much bigger than you."

"How much bigger than me? I'm pretty big you know."

"See that tree over there, see how high that first branch is," said Banna. "That is how big our elephants are in Africa. They are the largest land animals in the world."

"Their ears are huge and they flap them when they are cranky," said Bree, laughing.

"Honey! Are they telling the truth?" asked Emme.

"Yes, Emme," said Honey, amused.

"You have red bottoms," Emme said to Banna and Bree, who laughed at how direct and honest she was.

Banna chuckled. "Honey! Is Emme telling the truth?"

"Definitely!" said Honey laughing. "There are no redder bottoms here!"

Emme laughed and flapped her trunk around not realising how strong she was. She knocked Banna and Bree to the ground. She was still a baby, although she was bigger than Banna and Bree. Unable to realise her size and strength, she could be a little clumsy at times.

"Oops, that trunk has a mind of its own when I'm laughing," she said giggling, and then she helped them get back up off the ground.

Chapter 5

One day, all the animals decided to go down to the river to cool off. Rani, a female orangutan and Remi, her baby, came over from the adjoining unprotected forest beside the one they were in. Just like Emme, Remi was bigger than Banna and Bree, and she was only a baby. Esther and Emme came lumbering through the forest knocking down the plants and foliage as they went. The proboscis monkeys, as well as the hornbills and orangutans, came to the river's edge to play.

"Mum, let's make a wave," said Emme mischievously.

Esther and Emme ran as fast as they could to the edge of the river to see how big a wave they could make as they crashed into the water below. They trumpeted all the way to the water's edge. Everybody laughed as the pygmy elephants hit the water and sent a huge wave rippling down the river.

"Surfs up," said Pedro to Paige. "Do you want to go surfing?"

Pedro and Paige sat on short logs in the water and tried to surf the waves Emme and Esther made.

Rani and Remi watched from the bank cautiously as the other animals played. The animals cheered at the size of the waves they made, and they cheered louder if the wave was huge. Then Esther and Emme would suck the water up into their trunks and spray the animals on the bank. Remi laughed as the water soaked into her orange fur cooling her down.

Hope and Honey, the hornbills, sat in the branches above the river trying to hide from the spray of water, but Emme was very careful to include everyone in her water soaking. Hope and Honey squawked and flapped their wings every time they were sprayed.

"Remi, come in the water," pleaded Emme. "You can sit on my back." Remi, the baby orangutan, ran over to Emme and jumped onto her back.

"Emme," said Rani protectively. "Just go gently please; Remi is not a confident swimmer."

"Mum, I'll be okay," said Remi. Soon, the baby orangutan was holding onto Emme's back as she bounced around. Remi laughed as they ran to the water's edge, and laughed even harder when occasionally she was thrown off Emme's back, over her head and into the river. Emme scooped her up every time and put her back onto her back.

"Bree, come and play with me on Emme's back," pleaded Remi.

"I'm not a great swimmer," said Bree.

"Come on, Bree," Emme called out to Bree. "Has one of those African elephants ever ridden into the water with you on their backs? This little tiny elephant won't let you drown!" Emme moved out of the deeper water and came over to the bank so Bree could hop on her back.

"How can I say no to you two?" said Bree. As she turned to hop on Emme's back, she whispered to Banna, "Keep two eyes on me, Banna; I don't feel like drowning today."

Banna watched Bree hop onto Emme's back and remembered a time back in Australia when Bree nearly drowned. He knew how nervous Bree must be.

"Not on my watch, Bree," said Banna to Bree. "I'll keep you safe."

Bree held onto Emme's back and laughed with Remi as they charged towards the river bank. Each time, Remi and Bree were flipped into the water over Emme's head. As soon as they hit the water, Emme would scoop them back up with her trunk. The other orangutans on the bank cheered at every flip.

"That looks awesome!" yelled Banna to Bree.

"It is!" Remi squealed.

"Hop on with us!" yelled Bree.

"Come on, Banna," said Emme. "Get on my

back so you can go home and tell all those ele-phants as big as the trees how much fun pigmy elephants are." She moved closer to the riverbank so Banna could crawl onto her back.

Soon, Remi, Banna and Bree were all sitting on Emme's back as she charged for the water's edge. They hurtled over Emme's head and into the water, only to be scooped up in her trunk and placed on her back to start over again. The animals enjoyed a wonderful day together, and Bree and Banna could not remember laughing so hard in a very long time. They laughed until their stomachs hurt.

That night, the animals from the reserve sat around talking late into the night and quickly became good friends. They met the other mon-keys in the jungle who weren't a lot different from the monkeys in Botswana, and were just as cheeky.

Chapter 6

The next day, Bree and Banna were in the clearing with Pedro when they saw a lot of smoke in the distance.

"That smoke is very close," said Pedro. "Most fires are lit for land clearing purposes. I wonder how close to our reserve that is."

"Do you want to go and see how close it is?" asked Banna.

"I think that might be a good idea, just to make sure it is not in one of our neighbouring reserves."

Pedro, Banna and Bree hurried off into the jungle. They scampered through the forest amongst the treetops and along the forest floor.

"The forest over there is on fire," said Banna. "Is that a neighbouring reserve?"

"No, that is the forest where Rani and Remi live," said Pedro, frowning. "Their forest isn't a government reserve, so it isn't as safe."

"Oh no! I hope they are safe!" cried Bree. "Do you get many fires?"

"More and more plantations are planted all the time," said Pedro. "As long as there is demand for palm oil, there will be deforestation and the destruction of our habitat."

"Don't people care about the endangered animals?" asked Bree. "Surely, when they have animals like the proboscis monkeys that can't be found anywhere else in the world, they want to take special care of them."

"The plantation farmers like the money more," said Pedro.

They went along the boundary of the reserve, checking that no damage had been done. They saw the rangers in the forest looking for fires.

"We are lucky to have the rangers to protect our reserve," said Pedro. "I wouldn't live anywhere else; it isn't safe."

"Why does Rani live in her forest when it is not protected?" asked Banna.

"She was bought up there and it is her home," said Pedro. "Orangutans lived throughout the Borneo forests many years ago. There were many forests and they were dense and beautiful. As the demand for palm oil increased, the orangutan population decreased."

"And all for biscuits and shampoo," said Bree softly.

"I think we can go back home now," said Pedro. "The rangers are checking on the reserves, so they will be watching where the fires are burning."

They were just about to turn back to go home to their friends, when they heard sobs in the treetops above them. They looked up into the branches to see Rani. Baby Remil was not to be seen. Bree, Banna and Pedro quickly climbed up the tree to find the large, orange, hairy orangutan out of breath and crying.

"Rani, what's wrong?" asked Pedro. "Where is Remi? And why are you so far away from your rainforest?"

"Oh Pedro," cried Rani between sobs. "There was a fire in our rainforest and people were cutting down the trees. Remi and I were separated in the noise, smoke and confusion. She is only a baby and I don't know where she is."

Pedro turned to Banna and Bree, "This is what I was telling you about. They burn the forests that we live in to turn them into plantations. Animals die every day here, especially the orangutans. If they catch Remi, they will kill her or sell her on the illegal pet trade market to get some extra money."

"What are illegal pet markets?" asked Banna.

"They sell captured animals for an enormous profit to buyers from all around the world," said Pedro, who was looking at the sobbing, hunched over Rani.

"Then we have to find her," said Bree firmly.

"Rani, come with us," said Pedro gently. "We will set off the horn of Borneo and get some search parties organised to find Remi."

The four friends moved as fast as they could through the forest and back to where the other animals were waiting.

Chapter 7

When Pedro returned, he sent a little leaf monkey off to find the hornbills. Hope and Honey arrived almost immediately.

"Honey, sound the horn of Borneo," said Pedro, clearly in command. "We need the aviation squad ready for immediate dispatch."

The sound of a longhorn echoed through the reserve. The ground shook as the herds of pygmy elephants crashed through into the clearing. The branches of trees rustled as proboscis monkeys, gibbons, leaf monkeys, and macaques appeared and then dropped to the ground. Within minutes, animals of all sizes and shapes gathered around Pedro.

Honey, the black hornbill, called everyone to attention, and then Pedro started the meeting with the animals in the reserve.

"We have all seen the smoke in the forest today," said Pedro loudly, so everyone could hear him. "Remi has gone missing in the smoke and confusion."

Collective gasps of shock at the news could be heard, and the other orangutans moved in to comfort Rani. The native animals of Borneo knew the fate of orangutan babies separated from their mothers during fires and were aware that opportunist people would either kill them or sell them to the illegal pet trade.

"We need to assemble our search and rescue squads immediately so we can find Remi and bring her home to her mother," said Pedro.

Rani's quiet sobs could be heard as Pedro spoke.

"Honey, I want you to command the birds. We need every bird in the reserve, not just our normal search squad. I want immediate dispatch. Send them out into the neighbouring reserves and report back quickly on your findings. Hope, you stay here at the command post and everyone will report back to you at sundown."

"We are mobile," said Honey, starting to flap her wings.

Honey launched into flight, her huge wings gracefully flapping slowly, her body moving higher and higher into the sky. The sky came alive with the movement of the birds as they spread out to look for Remi.

"Pygmy elephants! I want you to scout the riverbanks," continued Pedro. "Follow the river up to the other reserves. Come back when you reach the edge of the unprotected reserves. Go no further than the unprotected reserves. The plantation farmers will kill pygmy elephants on sight, so be on high alert." The elephants trumpeted and thundered towards the river. Esther led the charge with baby Emme trumpeting by her side.

"Monkeys and gibbons!" he ordered. "Search the forest floors. You are quick and strong; cover as much area as you can before sundown. Paige, take the proboscis monkeys and glide through the treetops and look for Remi there," Pedro said. "Rupsa, gather Rani and the orangutans and go to all Remi's favourite places that you know she likes to go to in the reserves. Do not go outside the reserves! It is a dangerous time for orangutans!"

Poppy, a proboscis monkey, stayed to look after the baby animals at the home camp so they would be safe.

Bree and Banna searched with Pedro and Paige. They searched in the treetops and on the jungle floor. The birds flew out over the plantations and neighbouring forests and spread the word to the animals in the neighbouring reserves that little Remi was lost and alone.

Chapter 8

The sun started to set, and the animals began to make their way back to Hope at the command post.

"There is too much smoke," said Honey the Hornbill to Pedro as she flew in. "The people have the fire contained in Rani's rainforest, but it is difficult to see through the smoke. The birds try to fly low, but the smoke is dense and there is a lot of it. It isn't safe."

"It might settle by tomorrow so the birds can get in there and search," said Pedro.

The sun started to set and by nightfall the command post was busy with the returning animals that had searched all afternoon.

Rani was upset, and the other orangutans tried to get her to eat and sleep. They reassured her that they would find her baby.

At the end of the night, Pedro addressed the animals. "Thank you for searching all afternoon for Remi. Rest up tonight. We will begin searching again at first light and continue all day tomorrow."

"Should we widen the search?" asked Emme.

"Yes, tomorrow, monkeys, proboscis monkeys, gibbons, we need to go further into the surrounding reserves in case Remi is somewhere alone and afraid," said Pedro. "Birds, we need you back in the skies, so we can spot her as quickly as we can. Keep searching in the unprotected forests. Get back to the command post if you do."

At first light, the animals set out again to search for Remi in the surrounding forests. The next day turned into night and still there was no word about Remi. The animals regrouped again that night. Everyone was tired and disappointed that Remi had not been found.

Banna and Bree came upon Pedro in the camp that night, sitting on a log, alone. They went and sat with him. "Pedro," said Banna, "what if Remi is no longer in any of the reserves? The birds have searched for two days in the unprotected forests. The other animals have searched high and low in the reserves."

"I am starting to think the same thing, Banna," said Pedro sadly.

"What if we start searching closer to the roadsides and home sites?" suggested Bree.

"That makes it very dangerous for the searchers," explained Pedro. "If they are on the roadside and near homes, they could be harmed by people or their machines. The chances of more of our searchers being hurt or killed will be higher."

"Then come with us, and the three of us will go and find Remi and bring her home to her mother," suggested Bree.

"You would do that for Remi?" asked Pedro.

"We have to try," explained Bree. "We have to try everything before we tell Rani that her baby is gone. Baboons live in big family groups called troupes. We understand what family means and how much this little one means to her mother."

"I'm coming too," said Paige, overhearing the conversation.

"And I am coming too," said Rupsa.

"You will need me to give you directions from the sky," said Honey from the branch above them.

"Okay," said Pedro relenting. "We will set off first thing in the morning, but only this small group, and we all stay together."

Chapter 9

Early the next morning, the animals began to search again in their assigned areas. Pedro, Banna, Bree, Paige, Rupsa and Honey set off to look for Remi outside the reserves, staying on the outskirts of the jungle. They saw people in uniforms that were there to protect the reserves and the orangutans. From the treetops, they could see the vehicles and dusty trucks moving along the gravel roads to and from the plantations.

After hours of watching trucks, they decided to move closer to the plantation homes. They moved through the tops of the trees and closer to the homes below. They had a great view of the houses and carefully checked each home before moving on to the next one.

There were other houses in the distance, so they decided to go further and inspect them all. They moved quietly through the treetops and closer to the people with their trucks. As they neared one of the houses, they could see what looked like cages on the veranda.

"We need to go down to the cages to see what is in there," said Banna.

"I'm small and quick," said Bree. "I will drop down and have a look."

"Be careful," said Banna. He knew he would not be able to stop her.

Bree quietly scampered down the tree, across the lawn of the yard and over to the cages. She looked inside them all. There was more than one orangutan in every cage. Most of them were babies. As she peered into the last cage, she saw Remi asleep on the floor of the cage.

"Remi," Bree whispered. "Remi, wake up." Remi did not stir.

"Remi," said Bree, a little louder. Remi's voice attracted the attention of the dog that came sniffing over. Banna looked up to see the dog running across the yard towards Bree. She scampered across the yard with the dog hot on her heels, and she climbed back up the tree to where the others were waiting.

"Remi is in the cage," said Bree. "There are many other orangutans in the cages, as well. They are babies, just like Remi."

"One of those babies is our Remi," said Pedro urgently. "We must get her out and the others, too."

"How do we get to them?" asked Paige.

"We have to unlock the cages," said Banna.

"No, that will take too long. We need to take the cages and work out how to unlock them later," suggested Paige.

"I think that is a great idea, Paige. Remi looks so weak; they all look weak, so if we can just get them out of there, they might be okay," said Bree.

"I think I should try to go back to the forest rangers," suggested Rupsa. "They will see me, and wonder why I am so far out of the reserves and follow me. They will be looking for orangutans, hurt or lost in the fire."

"Are you sure it's safe?" asked Bree.

"We have to do something," said Rupsa. "Far too many of my orangutan friends end up dead or injured because of deforestation, all to make way for palm oil plantations."

"I think that is a really good idea, Rupsa," said Honey nodding. "There are so many rangers around the reserves today because of the fire. They will be ready to help injured and lost orangutans."

"Remi knows me, so I will go down and talk to her," suggested Pedro. "I'll tell her we are going to get her out."

"If I can't get help, we will carry out the cage together when I get back," said Rupsa. "At least we know where she is now; we will get her out of here."

Pedro nodded in agreement. Rupsa moved across the treetops and back towards where they had seen the rangers.

Chapter 10

Pedro tried to enter the yard, but a scruffy, angry dog came growling at him. He scampered back up the tree.

"We have a problem with the dog," said Pedro, fear evident in his voice.

"I will distract him," said Bree. "Get down to Remi, see if you can wake her up and talk to her before the dog comes back."

Bree scampered along the edge of the yard, close enough to encourage the dog to chase her. The dog was faster than Bree had anticipated, and she wove in and out of the dense jungle with him right on her heels.

Pedro sneaked into the yard and gently spoke to Remi. "Remi, it's Pedro, wake up."

"Pedro?" said Remi, opening her eyes. "You found me! I can't get out of this cage. There was a fire in the forest, and we couldn't see. There was so much smoke. I don't know where Mum is. A man trapped me and locked me in this cage." She started to cry.

"Be brave, Remi. We are going to get you out of here and return you to your mum. Your mum is safe; she is looking for you. Stay awake so you know what is going on. Banna, Bree, Honey and Paige are up in the tree over there."

Although Remi was weak, she smiled at Pedro. Pedro tried to move the cage, but it was too heavy for one proboscis monkey. He pulled and pushed at the cage in vain.

"The cage is heavy," Pedro told Remi. "I will go and get some help, so we can get you home. I'll be back as soon as I can."

Remi nodded her head. "Okay," she whispered.

Pedro moved quickly across the yard and back up the tree to where Banna was keeping watch. "The cage is too heavy. I don't know how we are going to move it," he told the others.

"What about the orangutans?" suggested Banna.

"Good idea, but it is too dangerous if these people are illegal pet traders. I also think we will need even more muscle than just Rupsa, Rani, and the orangutans. Those cages are heavy, and we need to get the other baby orangutans out of the cages, as well."

Banna and Pedro looked at each other in the same instant. "The pygmy elephants!" they cried.

Banna knew Bree wasn't too far away as the dog had returned to the house.

"There doesn't appear to be anybody at home. We need to get Remi out now," said Pedro. He turned to Honey the Hornbill, "Honey, can you go back and find the pygmy elephants, please? Tell them where we are and that we need them quickly. Bring them here through the reserves as safely as possible."

"I will also remind them not to eat anything on the way," said Honey and flew away into the distance.

"Why can't they eat anything?" asked Banna.

"The plantation farmers bait the food around their plantations to keep the pygmy elephants away," said Paige. "They will kill them any way they can."

Bree scampered back up the tree and sat beside Banna. She was out of breath. "What has happened?" Banna and Pedro told her of their plan.

Bree, Banna, Pedro and Paige waited in the treetops above where the little orangutans were, and kept watch.

"That dog is faster than I thought it would be," said Bree. "I think my bottom is a shade redder than it usually is. It nipped me a few times."

"And I think Honey would say that you are telling the truth," said Banna smiling.

They all laughed. Then they sat and waited.

Chapter 11

Meanwhile, Rupsa continued to move slowly across the treetops, looking for the rangers. When he found them, he dropped onto the ground far enough away from them so that he wasn't too close.

One of the rangers saw him, and he and the other ranger started to follow him at a distance. Rupsa made the daring move to stay out in the clearing and walk down the road.

He slowly lumbered down the roads towards the driveway of the house where they had been.

The rangers continued to follow Rupsa at a distance, just to make sure he was safe and protected. They wondered why he was away from the protected areas and close to where the plantations were. The rangers had rung for backup and tranquilisers so they could get Rupsa back to a safe area. They just had to follow him until the other rangers arrived.

Honey flew into the reserve and back to the command post. There was no sign of Esther and Emme; just Poppy, the proboscis monkey looking after the monkey babies.

"Where are Esther and the pygmy elephants?" asked Honey.

"They are at the river. They have only just checked in and gone searching again so they aren't far away," said Poppy.

Honey flew to the river and found Esther, Emme, and the rest of the pygmy elephants having a drink.

"Esther!" squawked Honey.

"Hi, Honey," yelled Esther. "How is the search going? Have you found Remi?"

"Yes, we have found her and a lot of other baby

orangutans in cages. We need your strength to move the cages and get them all out of there."

"Sure, I will bring the herd," said Esther. "Where are we going?

"Remi is on a plantation. Only bring the elephants who want to come. We know how dangerous plantations are for pygmy elephants. Anyone who is afraid, stay here, and everyone will understand. You might want to leave Emme at home."

"I'm not staying at home!" cried Emme. "That is my friend in the cage, and I am going!"

"She can come," said Esther. "She will stay by my side."

Esther discussed the situation with the herd. They were unanimous; they all wanted to bring Remi home safely to her mother.

Esther threw her trunk into the air and trumpeted. The herd responded and trumpeted as well.

Esther and the rest of the pygmy herd followed Honey, trampling through the forest. Just before they arrived at the house, the elephants slowed down and quietly edged towards the clearing nearby.

Chapter 12

"**E**sther and the pygmy elephants are here at the edge of the forest," said Honey as she circled down and landed onto a branch. "I told them to be very careful. These people want them dead."

"The whole herd is here?" asked Pedro, surprised.

"Yes, they are all here," answered Honey. "They all wanted to help. They are ready to help the babies out of those cages."

"Good, let's go and take Remi and the other

orangutan babies home," said Pedro.

Pedro and Banna climbed down the tree and went to where the elephants were.

"Remi is in that big cage over there, and she looks very weak," Pedro told Esther. "There are other orangutan babies in the other cages. We need to push the cages off the veranda."

"That shouldn't be a problem," said Esther. "We have the whole herd to push."

"We need to push them out of the yard," said Banna to Esther. "Get them onto the road and see if you can push them down the road. Rupsa is trying to find the rangers."

"We will push them all the way home if we have to," said Esther.

Esther led the charge to the cages on the veranda. The dog started to run towards the elephants but changed its mind when he saw their size and their number. Banna and Pedro also ran towards the cages with the elephants. The big brown eyes of the orangutans were watching them with curiosity.

"Baby orangutans," said Pedro, "hold on tight, we are going to try to get you out of here."

"Hang on, babies," said Banna. "This ride is going to be a bit rocky."

"Emme, you are here," said Remi, a little surprised and confused.

"I'll get you out of here, Remi," said Emme to her friend, pushing the cage as hard as she could.

"Push, Emme, take me home!" Remi cried out.

Pedro spoke to the frightened baby orangutans again and told them to hold on tightly to their cages. Their eyes were wide with fear.

The elephants pulled and pushed the cages until they had moved them off the veranda and onto the grass. They shoved the cages again. They moved them off the grass and towards the driveway of the house.

"You are working well, pigmies!" encouraged Esther. "Let's take them home." The pygmy elephants continued to push the cages further down the driveway. The elephant herd pushed with all its might.

Rupsa bounded up the driveway, followed at a distance by the rangers. He started to run as he heard the cries of the baby orangutans.

The rangers looked ahead and rubbed their

53

eyes in astonishment at the sight of a herd of pygmy elephants pushing cages down the road. They got on their phones and their voices sounded urgent. They were still at quite a distance from Rupsa, but they could hear and see the baby orangutans in the cages. They started to move quickly up the driveway.

A vehicle with men in it from the plantation suddenly appeared from one of the back roads of the property.

"Pedro!" called Bree, "there is a vehicle coming up the back of the property towards the house!"

The vehicle sped into the yard and five men jumped out and started running after the elephants. They hit the elephants with big sticks trying to chase them away. Esther moved in between the men and Emme. The men savagely beat her with their sticks.

Rupsa was nearly at the cages.

"Rupsa, run, they have big sticks," called Banna. "And there are too many of them."

Rupsa became agitated, but kept running towards Remi and the baby orangutans and paced around the cages to protect them.

One of the men caught sight of Rupsa, moved away from the elephants and started bashing Rupsa with his stick. He hit Rupsa repeatedly until he collapsed.

"Kill it if you have to!" yelled one of the men. "Those babies are worth too much money to us to let them get away!"

Banna and Pedro ran to Rupsa, trying to shield him from the men with sticks.

"Kill these two as well! Kill them all!" the man yelled to the others.

The men turned from the elephants and started to hit Pedro and Banna. Pedro received blows to his stomach and legs, Banna to his eyes and head. Blood trickled down Banna's face, but he continued to crawl beside Rupsa to protect him. The elephants turned and saw what was happening. They regrouped and started to charge at the men. The men ran around them trying to hit them with their powerful sticks.

One of the rangers called out, "Put the sticks down, now!" The rangers pointed their revolvers at the men.

Chapter 13

The poachers were shocked to see the two forest rangers running up the driveway and getting closer to the cages.

Emme took her chance. While the poachers were distracted by the forest rangers running towards them, she charged at the poachers, knocking them to the ground. The men looked sheepish being knocked down by the baby of the herd. Emme turned around and ran at them again.

"Don't. Lock. My. Friend. In. A. Cage," she screamed as she crashed into them again. She stood over them, flapped her ears and trumpeted in rage.

Seeing the rangers holding up their guns, Pedro and Banna quickly scampered back up into the tree to hide in the branches. They were both bleeding and injured. Esther herded the pygmy elephants into the forest so they could see what was going on without being seen.

"Why do you have orangutan babies in those cages?" yelled a ranger at the poachers.

"I found them, and I was going to help them get stronger before I release them into the wild," answered one of the men. "I am looking after them."

"He's lying," said Honey. "I can spot a lie a mile away."

"Even I know he is lying," said Bree smiling.

"The orangutans are sick. How many days have you had them here?" asked the ranger.

"I have tried to feed them, but they won't eat," one of the men said.

"Tut, tut," said Honey, "another lie."

"I think you are all going to jail," said the ranger. "Orangutan babies are to be protected, not sold off to illegal pet trades."

A truck drove up the driveway and two men got out and ran over to the rangers. They looked incredulous when they were told of the situation that had just unfolded.

A ranger exchanged angry words with the poachers who had held Remi captive. Pedro seemed to think that the men who held Remi and the other little orangutans in the cages were in a lot of trouble. The four men lifted Remi in her cage on the back of the truck. One by one, the four men lifted all of the cages and put them into the back of the truck.

The rangers checked Rupsa over and helped him onto the truck. He was bleeding heavily and his body ached.

"Let's go and hide in the truck so we can go with Remi and Rupsa," suggested Banna to Pedro. "Paige, can you take Bree and go back to Rani and tell her we know where Remi is? Honey, come with us in case we need your directions to get home to Rani."

Pedro and Banna dropped from the branches and crept quietly into the back of the truck below. They hid behind the cages. Rupsa could see them and tried to help hide them behind him. Esther, Emme, and the herd saw Banna and Pedro get into the truck and were pleased they were with the baby orangutans.

Paige and Bree waited in the treetops. Bree saw the writing on the door of the truck which said, "Sepilok Orangutan Centre," and the rangers tying the men's hands behind their backs.

After the truck drove off, Paige and Bree scampered as fast as they could back to the pygmy elephants and then back to the other animals at the command post. They found Rani waiting there.

Chapter 14

"Rani, Remi has been found," said Paige. Rani's tear-streaked face lit up with the good news.

"Rupsa, Pedro and Banna are with her in the truck," Bree told her. "They are going with her so we know where she is, and where they have taken her. Then they will come back and show you."

"Truck?" asked Rani. "What truck?"

"We found her at a plantation in a cage with other baby orangutans," said Bree. "The rangers sent her off in a truck. I think they are helping her."

"She also has Pedro, Rupsa and Banna with her, so she is not alone," said Rani softly.

"Now I have hope."

"What kind of truck was it?" asked Poppy, one of the female proboscis monkeys.

"It was big, with a tray on the back, and there was writing on the door that said 'Sepilok Orangutan Centre.' I wonder what they do with the orangutans there."

"I know where they are!" screeched Hope. "There is a special place not far from here that looks after injured orangutans. They nurse them and release them into a special reserve where they are safe."

"Do you know how to get there?" asked Rani.

"Of course I do!" beamed Hope. "Follow me."

Bree, Paige, Rani and Hope quickly set off to find the orangutan centre.

Meanwhile, back in the dusty, bumpy truck, Pedro was able to reach Remi's cage. He tried to talk to Remi, but he couldn't get her to wake up.

The truck stopped at a big building. People

rushed out and cut the locks on the cages. There were many people who came outside and picked up the baby orangutans and took them back inside. Rupsa was helped into the building. They looked at his wounds and patched him up. They gave him some food and water.

Pedro and Banna climbed quietly into the trees and tried to work out how they could get Remi away and back to her mother.

"We will have to wait until nightfall," said Pedro.

Chapter 15

Banna and Pedro watched through the windows from the treetops. They could see the people gently lifting the limp baby orangutans into a special, dimly lit room. They looked down the throats of the baby orangutans, into their eyes, and listened to their chests. They inserted needles into them and put tubes into their arms.

After a long time, Remi's eyes began to slowly open. She looked very weak, and they gave her a bottle with liquid in it. She sucked it slowly at first. It wasn't the same as her mum's milk, but she was hungry and she started to gulp the milk. After a few hours, the nurses were able to take the tubes out of Remi's arms and hold her as her mum did.

"They are trying to help them," said Pedro. "Look, some of them are opening their eyes and looking around."

"Remi has opened her eyes," said Banna. "The people are making her well, and they really care."

Rupsa went over to Remi, and Remi crawled into his arms and lay there.

Banna and Pedro realised that Remi was going to be okay. They were so happy they nearly fell off their branch in excitement.

"As soon as she is a little stronger, we'll get them out of here," said Pedro.

"There you are," said Bree happily to Banna as she climbed onto the branch beside him.

"How did you know where to come?" asked Banna, surprised.

"I saw the writing on the truck and Hope knew where it was."

Bree, Rani and Hope settled onto the tree branch beside Pedro and Banna. When Rani looked down and saw little Remi lying in Rupsa's arms, she started to cry.

"She is okay, Rani. We have been with her the whole time," said Pedro. "The people are helping her and making her stronger. She was so weak when she got here."

"Thank you so much, my friends, for staying with Remi and bringing her back safely," said Rani.

Rani wanted her baby and she wanted her baby now. She climbed down the tree and lumbered over to the building where Remi was. The people turned to see the big mother orangutan and knew at once that this was Remi's mother by the way Remi's eyes lit up when she saw her. A lady coaxed Rani gently into the room and reunited her with her baby. Remi reached for her mother and gently nestled into her arms.

Little tears of joy ran down the faces of those watching from the treetops. Even the people who had helped the tiny orangutans were tearful.

Pedro, Paige, Banna, Bree and Hope started their journey back to the other animals.

They returned to the clearing, and the animals of the forest were waiting for news of Rani and Remi. Emme ran up to Banna and Pedro and asked if Remi was all right. Honey could see that Banna and Pedro were still wounded, so she took it upon herself to make the announcement. "Remi has been reunited with her mother. They are at the orangutan centre with all the other babies that were found."

The animals were happy that Remi was safe and that there were fewer babies being sold on the illegal pet trade.

"Now, to clean you up Pedro and Banna," said Paige. "You both look terrible."

The leaf monkeys helped clean Banna and Pedro up. They wiped the blood from Pedro and Banna's fur and wrapped their injuries in warm leaves so they would heal. Pedro and Banna moved away from the excited animals and fell into a deep sleep.

Bree found Banna sleeping and lay beside him to keep an eye on him.

The next morning, the sun appeared in the sky and Banna woke to see Bree sitting beside him. She had water for him to drink and had washed his fur again.

Pedro walked over to them. He looked a lot better than he did the night before. "I was thinking I might go and see how Rani, Rupsa and Remi are feeling this morning. Would you both like to come?"

"I would love to!" said Emme, who had been watching Banna from the bushes.

"You need to check that is okay with you mum first," said Pedro to Emme.

"I have already asked her. I was waiting until you all woke up, so you could take me," replied Emme with a huge grin on her face.

"I'm coming too," said Honey from the branch above them.

"We're all going to see Remi," said Emme excitedly.

"You were a hero yesterday," said Banna to Emme, standing up and moving over to her. "You fought as hard, maybe even harder than any of us, and you are a baby. I think you are special, Emme; one very courageous little pygmy elephant."

Emme moved to give him a hug with her trunk, but knocked him over. "Sorry Banna, I wanted to hug you, but my trunk got in the way."

Everyone laughed.

"Let's go!" said Emme.

Chapter 16

Pedro, Banna, Honey, Bree and Emme moved through the reserve to the Sepilok Orangutan Centre. Emme and Bree stayed at the edge of the reserve while Pedro and Banna climbed the tree to look inside the room.

"They aren't in there," said Banna, surprised.

"They must be out in the sanctuary," said Pedro.

"Let me fly over the sanctuary and see where they are," said Honey. Honey flew over the sanctuary and saw Rani with Remi in her arms, and circled down to land beside them.

"Rani, how are you feeling?" asked Honey.

"We are both happy and healthy," said Rani.

"You have some visitors to see you both. Wait at the fence of the sanctuary, and I'll go and get them and tell them where to meet you."

"What a wonderful surprise!" said Rani, moving towards the fence.

Within minutes of arriving at the fence, they saw their friends on the other side.

"Remi!" yelled Emme in excitement. Remi looked up. She had a huge smile on her face; she knew that voice.

"Emme, it is so good to see you. I miss you already," said Remi.

"What do you mean? When do you come back to the reserve?" asked Emme.

"We won't be coming back to the reserve," said Rani. "This is our home now. Our home has been burned to the ground, but we are safe here and the sanctuary is huge. I don't have to worry about us getting hurt anymore."

"But can you get out to come and play with me?" asked Emme.

"No," said Remi. "We can still be friends and

you could come and visit me."

"It won't be the same," said Emme. "I can't run into the river here with you on my back."

"Who are you talking to, Remi?" asked another baby orangutan who had followed her over.

"They are my friends," said Remi. "This is Emme, and she helped saved my life yesterday. She helped rescue all the baby orang-tans from the cages."

"She's a hero!" gushed the baby orangutan.

"It is so good to see you looking healthy, Remi," said Bree. "Are those your friends playing over there on the ropes?"

"Yes, they are my friends," said Remi. "They are really nice. Some of them have been here a long time and others arrived yesterday with me. They all seem like a lot of fun."

"That one has a bucket on his head," said Emme laughing.

"He is a funny fellow," said Remi. "He was in the cages with me. He will stay here where it is safe and hopefully they will find his mum like I did."

"I will fly over to the neighbouring reserves

and forests and get the word out there that the baby orangutans have been found," said Honey.

"Thank you, Honey," said Rani. "There are a few orangutan mothers who don't know where their babies are."

"I will come and visit you, Rani," said Pedro. "I'm sure many of the animals will."

Rupsa ambled over.

"Rupsa!" yelled Emme. "You look much better today; there is not as much blood on you."

"Emme!" yelled Rupsa. "Our little elephant hero who helped saved Remi!"

Emme blushed.

"Are you staying here too, my friend?" asked Pedro.

"Yes, Pedro, it is safe here, and they look after us. There are so many babies who don't have parents; I would like to help them. Look at the little ones playing after what happened yesterday. Besides, the people here are kind and care about our safety."

"We will visit you," said Pedro. "At least, here your habitat is safe; no one can burn it down or cut down the trees."

"Deforestation continues to be the biggest problem for orangutans," said Rupsa, "but I have found my home, and I don't have to worry every day that it will be my last."

"Thank you to all of you," said Rani. "Without you all, I wouldn't have Remi back with me and be living in this beautiful place."

"Oh, I want to hug you," wailed Emme.

Banna chuckled. "You are safer on that side of the fence," he said to Rani. "She is dangerous when she tries to hug you."

Emme chased Banna around trying to hug him.

They talked for a couple of hours and then headed back to their home.

Banna and Bree had settled down with the other animals and were talking about the events of the last few days when they saw the familiar whirly wind and knew their journey to Borneo was ending.

"It is time for us to go, Pedro," said Bree.

"Please stay tonight," pleaded Pedro. "It won't be the same without the two of you. Without you, we would never have gone to that house and found Remi."

"We would love to," said Banna, "but when the winds blow we have to go home with it to our families. This journey will stay with us for a lifetime as will the memories of our Sabah adventure and your friendship, Pedro."

"The animals here are so supportive of each other," said Bree. "It's a wonderful place to live; keep protecting it as fiercely as you do."

Banna and Bree hugged each of their new friends. Emme came bounding towards them with her trunk swinging. She stopped and gently wrapped her trunk around them both and hugged them tightly.

And without another word spoken, the winds quickly whipped up into a storm. The leaves blew around their faces. They shut their eyes.

The familiar voice began to speak, "Banna and Bree, it is time to go home, but what an adventure you have had. Some of these animals you have befriended are endangered, and without the help of the people you saw, may one day be extinct. Deforestation is a huge problem in Borneo and sadly, the orangutans numbers continue to dwindle every day. Treasure the time spent with the proboscis monkeys as you will not find a proboscis monkey anywhere else in the world other than the jungles of Borneo. This adventure was special because of the way you all worked together to unite Remi with her mother. Goodbye, Banna and Bree, until the next time the wind blows…"

THE END